THE ANIMALS OF FARTHING WOOD

The Adventures of Badger
in Winter

Colin Dann
Adapted by Clare Dannatt
Licensed by BBC Enterprises Ltd

RED FOX

Badger could feel in his bones that winter in White Deer Park was going to be very cold. Soon there was thick snow on the ground and nothing for the animals to eat.

Badger tried to sleep in his sett but it was cold even there, underground. 'Better go and see how my friends are,' he thought to himself. Badger was one of the animals of Farthing Wood who had travelled to the Park to find safety, and the Farthing Wood animals still looked after one another.

But it would have been better if Badger had stayed at home that night.

The Park was silent and empty. Badger struggled through the thick, icy, snow drifts.

'Perhaps I should go back,' he shivered.

Suddenly he felt himself slipping and sliding, and then falling. As Badger landed with a thump, pain shot through his leg. Badger tried to stand up – but he couldn't move. His leg was broken.

'Help! Help!' cried Badger weakly, but no one heard him. More snow started to fall and began to cover poor Badger, muffling his cries and hiding him.

'I can't find Badger,' Mole wailed to Fox. 'He's been gone for ages!'

Although the animals of Farthing Wood were thin and weak from hunger, they decided to search for Badger. Hare and Fox ran through the silent woods, and Kestrel hovered above the Park. But not even Kestrel with her keen sight could spot Badger. Was he buried in the snow?

Badger was covered by snow. But as he lay there, a human shadow suddenly passed over him. The Park Warden!

The Warden touched Badger, and felt that he was still breathing and warm – just. He pulled Badger out and carried him away. Badger was saved!

Badger was dreaming that he was dozing in the spring sunshine in the old Farthing Wood. 'I don't want to wake up in the snow,' he thought.

But when he did wake, Badger still felt warm. He opened his eyes and saw a fire burning brightly, and a bowl of milk in front of him. His leg was bandaged.

A grey cat was watching him. 'Hello, my name is Charlie. Welcome to the Warden's cottage,' it said.

Poor Mole did not know that Badger was safe. He crept around the Park, crying and calling for his friend. None of the other animals were out in the cold. They had given up the search. But Mole kept going.

'I'll never give up! Never!' he promised.

Badger lay comfortably in his warm basket, but he hadn't forgotten Mole.

'Better be getting back now,' he murmured. He started to his feet. Ouch! His leg gave way under him.

'Silly!' purred the grey cat. 'It'll be ages before you can go home.'

'But my friends will be worried about me,' wailed Badger.

'Friends?' asked the cat, curiously.

'Yes,' said Badger. 'I'm one of the animals of Farthing Wood...'

And as the snowflakes fell against the window and the fire crackled, Badger told Charlie the story of his travels.

'So,' said Badger when he finished his story, 'my friends mean a lot to me. And I need someone to take a message to them.'

'Not me!' said Charlie quickly.

But Badger talked him into it. Soon the cat was picking his way through the snow.

Mole dived into a tunnel when he saw a cat approaching.

'Stop!' miaowed Charlie. 'Are you Badger's friend? I've come to tell you he's safe and well.'

'Oh thank you! Thank you!' cried Mole, bursting into tears all over again.

Badger's leg got better day by day. One evening the Warden took off the bandage. Badger could walk again. It was time to go back to his friends.

But the cottage was very cosy. Badger shivered when he thought of all the ice outside. He licked his dinner bowl carefully. There was no food at home!

Badger knew he would have to go soon. He took a big breath, and set off through the snow.

Badger wandered sadly through White Deer Park. Where were his friends? By the time he saw Mole, he was tired and in a bad mood.

'Badger!' cried Mole happily. 'I knew you'd be back soon!'

Badger grunted. He was too cold to say much. Poor Mole watched his friend brush past him, looking for Fox.

Badger talked very strangely. He said it would be better for all the Farthing Wood animals to go and live in the Warden's cottage.

'It would be the end of our problems!' he insisted. 'We'd never go hungry or be cold again!'

His friends stared at him as if he were mad.

'We're wild creatures,' said Fox, gently. 'We can't live in houses. Go home to your sett, Badger, and have a good sleep. You'll feel better in the morning.'

'All right then,' answered Badger crossly. 'I will go home – but not to my sett. I'm going back to the Warden's cottage.'

It was a long way back to the Warden's cottage, but Badger plodded on.

'They don't know what's good for them, that Farthing Wood lot,' he muttered. At last he arrived at the cottage door.

But instead of welcoming him back, the Warden gently shooed Badger away.

'Your friends will miss you,' said Charlie from the doorway. 'Don't forget your home in the wild.'

'Oh yes – of course,' mumbled Badger slowly, as if he'd just woken from a deep sleep.

And he turned around and headed towards his old sett and his friends.

'Welcome back, Badger!' cried the animals, Mole loudest of all.

'Sorry I was so silly,' muttered Badger.

'Think nothing of it, old friend,' said Fox warmly.

Badger smiled contentedly. It seemed a long time ago that he had set out to look for his friends, and broken his leg in the snow. At last he had found everyone again!

A RED FOX BOOK
Published by Random House Children's Books
20 Vauxhall Bridge Road, London SW1V 2SA

A division of Random House UK Ltd
London   Melbourne   Sydney   Auckland   Johannesburg
and agencies throughout the world

Text © Random House UK Ltd 1995
Illustrations by Arkadia. © 1995 Random House Children's Books
Licensed by BBC Enterprises Ltd

Animals of Farthing Wood Logotype © European
Broadcasting Union 1992. Licensed by BBC Enterprises Ltd
The Animals of Farthing Wood logotype is a trade mark
of BBC Enterprises Ltd and is used under licence.

First published by Red Fox 1995

Based on the animation series produced by
Telemagination/La Fabrique for the European Broadcasting Union
from the series of books about
The Animals of Farthing Wood by Colin Dann

Printed and bound in Great Britain
by BPC Paulton Books Ltd, Paulton, Bristol

RANDOM HOUSE UK limited Reg. No. 954009.

ISBN 0 09 937021 2